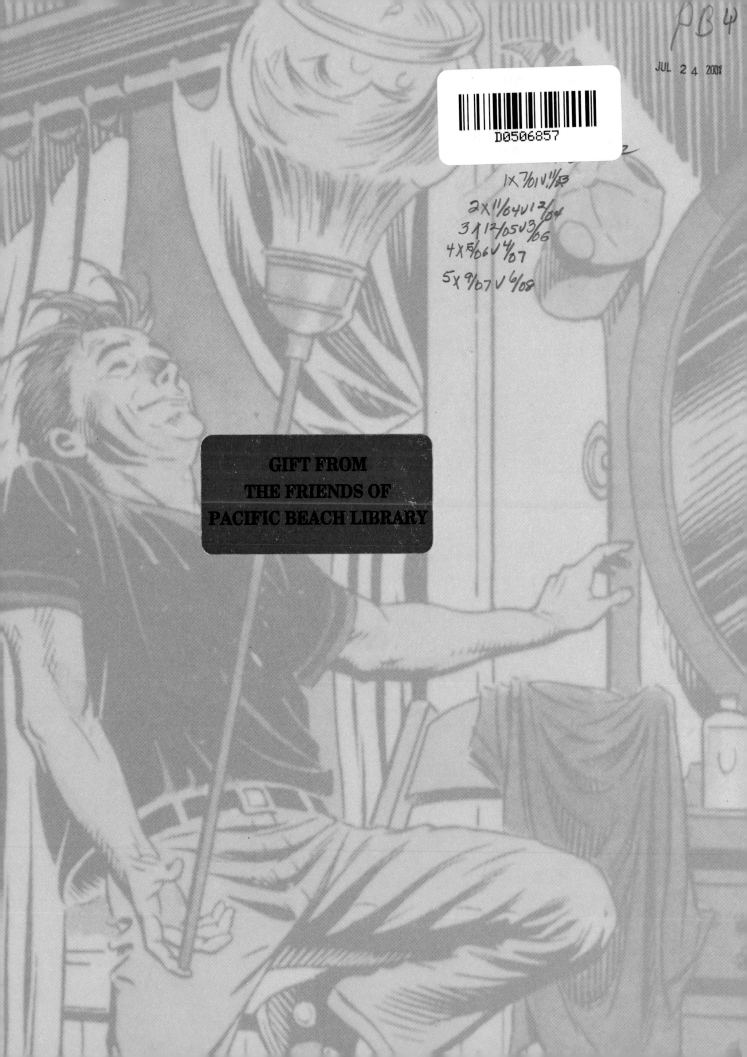

CONFESSIONS
OF A
CEREAL EATER!
BY
ROB MAISCH

B. HAMPTON

S. HAMPTON

HOLMES

PLUNKETT

DEDICATED WITH LOVE TO:
My wife Kristene
My sons, Dave and Scott
My parents, Fred and Madge
My brothers, Michael and Jeffrey and their families.

SPECIAL THANKS TO:
Jeff Tefft, Rick Johnston, Bob Arcand, Dave Conner, Tom Woolsey, Kyle
Rodriguez, Gary Gore, Terrie O'Neill, Marty Lakatos, Laura Sandin, Jamie
Gherman, Angie and Tom Slayton and the entire Hampton clan
for propping me up and making me smile through the good times and
bad over these many years.

Library of Congress catalog card # 95-71765
ISBN 1-56163-141-8
ISBN signed edition 1-56163-142-6
©1995 Rob Maisch
"Slow Dance" & "Klingon Battle Helmet" ©1995 Scott Hampton
"Mean Old Man" ©1995 Rand Holmes
"Griffin Love & The Hooker" ©1995 Sandy Plunhett
"Back in the Saddle" ©1995 Bo Hampton
Lettering by Tracy Hampton-Munsey
Edited by Letitia Glozer
Printed in Hong Kong

5 4 3 2 1

ComicsLit is an imprint and trademark of

NANTIER · BEALL · MINOUSTCHINE
Publishing inc.
new york

INTRODUCTION

This is my life. Bits and pieces of it, at any rate. These tales reflect a parade of characters and incidents that made me laugh as I meandered from mis-spent youth to addled adulthood over a period of roughly thirty years.

My good friend Scott Hampton first heard these stories over marathon games of Monopoly and Trivial Pursuit a dozen years ago in Columbia, South Carolina. He encouraged me to commit them to writing and offered his considerable artistic talents as well as those of some of the best illustrators in the Comics business to this book. I thank him for his vision and his friendship. We all should have such good "budds"! It's been a great project and we laughed a lot.

I hope you too, dear reader, will laugh a lot! Everyone has their own take on the Sixties and the decades that have followed. For me those years served only as a backdrop of fads, manners and mores to the *people* who fill these pages and the events in which we were involved during any moment in time. Along the way I got to be a son, brother, husband (twice!), father and friend in a host of locales and time periods. To quote The Grateful Dead, "What a long, strange trip it's been." Join me for the journey within these pages.

Rob "Rocco" Maisch
Somewhere in Cleveland
August, 1995

CONTENTS

THERE'S SOMETHING ABOUT THE AMBIENCE OF A GYMNASIUM THAT IS FUNDAMENTALLY AT ODDS WITH THE ATMOSPHERE DESIRED FOR A SCHOOL DANCE. NO MATTER HOW MUCH CREPE PAPER IS HUNG, THE SWEAT OF SEVERAL THOUSAND BALL GAMES AND A MILLION INDIVIDUAL SQUAT THRUSTS IN PHYS-ED CLASSES PERMEATES EVERY INCH OF THE HARDWOOD AND BRICK SURFACES.

STILL, THE CHANCE FOR SOME PURELY SOCIAL CONTACT WITH GIRLS HELD POWERFUL ALLURE AT FOURTEEN YEARS OF AGE, NO MATTER HOW CRUMMY THE SURROUNDINGS.

ROB + D.J.

"IN"

Slow Dance

GUYS ALWAYS HUNG OUT IN GROUPS OF TWO OR FOUR, THE OBJECT BEING TO PROVE THAT YOU HAD AT LEAST ONE FRIEND IN THE WORLD.

GIRLS WENT FOR AN ODD NUMBER—MINIMUM THREE, USUALLY SEVEN—WITH NO CAP ON THE TOP END. THEN THERE WAS THE STRANGE PACT AMONG FEMALES THAT ANY ATTRACTIVE GIRL MUST BE ACCOMPANIED BY TWO MONGREL FRIENDS *AT ALL TIMES.*

I SUSPECT THIS CONFIGURATION DERIVES FROM THE UNWRITTEN LAW THAT STATES "ANY BABE WHO IS NOT INTERESTED IN A GUY MAY CHEERFULLY HAND HIM OFF TO ONE OF HER KEN-L-RATION BUDDIES."

AND MANY MALE PAIRS WALKED AN ENDLESS CIRCLE OF THE COURT'S OUTER PERIMETER WITHOUT ONCE MAKING AN APPROACH...

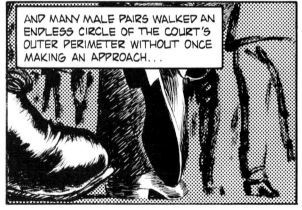

...BECAUSE ENDING UP WITH A CREATURE ON YOUR ARM WASN'T THE WORST THING THAT COULD HAPPEN. THERE WAS ALWAYS THE POSSIBILITY OF...

MASS REJECTION!!!

WE ALL THINK YOU SMELL

AS D.J. AND I JOINED THE RANKS OF THE WALKING DEAD I KEPT ONE EAR COCKED FOR A SLOW DANCE. NONE SEEMED FORTHCOMING AS "LAST TRAIN TO CLARKSVILLE," "YELLOW SUBMARINE" AND "YOU CAN'T HURRY LOVE" CAME RATTLING OUT OF THE TINNY SPEAKERS IN RAPID SUCCESSION.

THE SUPREMES PLAYED OUT AND BOPPIN' BOBBY COZIED UP TO HIS MICROPHONE AGAIN.

OK! OK! LET'S SLOW THINGS DOWN WITH THE LEFT BANKE! IT'S "LADIES' CHOICE" ON THIS ONE, SO DON'T YOU WALK AWAY... RENEE!!

NAIVE AND STUPID AS WE WERE, BECKER AND I BELIEVED THAT A "LADIES' CHOICE" WAS ABSOLUTE LAW AND THAT WE *COULD NOT*, WITHOUT RISKING PENALTIES UNKNOWN, ASK ANYONE TO DANCE.

DO YOU TWO WANT TO DANCE?

IT'S HARD TO SAY WHICH OF THEM LOOKED WORSE—TRUDY MOCHA OF THE SPARKLEY CAT GLASSES AND THE PROTRUDING BUCK TEETH...

...OR MARLEEN GOZA, WHO ALWAYS HAD SALIVA THE CONSISTENCY OF ELMER'S GLUE WELLING IN THE CORNER OF HER MOUTH.

UH... SORRY, GIRLS, WE PROMISED TO MEET SOME GUYS IN THE PING-PONG ROOM.

WE BEAT A HASTY RETREAT WHILE THEY GAZED OUT ONTO THE DANCE FLOOR, WHERE THE GOOD-LOOKING MEMBER OF THEIR TRIO WAS DANCING CROTCH-TO-CROTCH WITH THE JUNIOR VARSITY FOOTBALL CAPTAIN.

MAN, THAT WAS CLOSE!

ARE WE REALLY GONNA GO TO THE PING-PONG ROOM?

HELL, NO! JESUS! ONLY THE BIGGEST DINKS AND LOSERS HANG OUT IN THE PING-PONG ROOM!

BUT I WANTED TO PLAY PING-PONG.

FORGET IT! YOU'LL CATCH DINK COOTIES!

I GOT THE NEW AURORA MONSTER MODEL KIT YESTERDAY!

WHICH ONE?

"THE BRIDE OF FRANKENSTEIN." SHE'S ON THAT COOL OPERATING TABLE WITH THE ELECTRICAL TURBINES, JUST LIKE IN THE MOVIE!

COOL!

AND SO WE YAKKED IT UP FOR TEN MINUTES OR SO, GIVING TRUDY AND MARLEEN TIME TO FIND OTHER VICTIMS.

SHE'S GOING STEADY WITH HIM?!?

HAVE YOU GOT ANY MIDOL IN YOUR PURSE?

...WELL, I SAY SHE'S STUFFING IT! I'VE SEEN HER IN THE SHOWER!

HE KEEPS RIDING BY MY HOUSE ON HIS STUPID BIKE! YECCH!!!

SHE THINKS SHE'S SO COOL CUZ HER PARENTS BELONG TO THE COUNTRY CLUB!

HE GAVE HER A COKE WITH AN ASPIRIN IN IT! SHE GOT SO DRUNK!

I HEARD SHE'S P.G.!!

SO, I SAID HERE'S YOUR RING BACK, YOU BIG FINK!

PATTY! IS THAT A HICKEY ON YOUR NECK?!?

GIRL'S LAVATORY

AS WE WERE PASSING THE BOY'S LAVATORY WE HEARD MUFFLED SCREAMS AND THE SOUND OF A SCUFFLE JUST BEFORE THE DOOR BANGED OPEN AND A PAIR OF CUFFED PANTS SAILED IN FRONT OF US, SMACKING AGAINST SOME LOCKERS.

WONDER WHO'S GETTING PANTSED?

THE ANSWER CAME A HALF SECOND LATER AS DANNY WINSTON LURCHED INTO THE HALL CLAD IN HIS BVD'S, HIS HEAD SNAPPING LEFT AND RIGHT AS HE SCANNED FOR ONCOMING GIRLS.

BEFORE HE COULD REACH HIS PANTS, SEVERAL SCHOOL HOODS DRAGGED HIM BACK INTO A STALL TO GIVE HIM A SWIRLY.

HE SHOULDA LET DORN COPY OFF HIS ALGEBRA QUIZ TODAY.

BOYS LAVAT

YEAH, JUST BEING A BRAIN IS ENOUGH TO GET YOU PANTSED. REFUSING TO LET A BUTT-HOLE LIKE DORN COPY YOUR TEST IS STRAIGHT SUICIDE.

LET'S HEAD BACK TO THE GYM AND SEE WHAT'S GOING ON.

THE DANCE HAD MOVED INTO "PHASE 2" OF THE UNOFFICIAL 3-PHASE TEENAGE PARTY PROCESS WHILE WE WERE ABSENT. PHASE 1 WAS THE "FIRST LOOK" SEGMENT, WHICH USUALLY LASTED ROUGHLY 45 MINUTES. PHASE 2, A THIRTY-MINUTE TIME BLOCK, COULD BE TERMED THE "CAUTIOUS APPROACH" PERIOD. AT THIS JUNCTURE BOTH GENDERS TAKE A SERIOUS LOOK AROUND THE ROOM TO SIZE UP POSSIBLE CANDIDATES. WORKING UP THE GUTS TO APPROACH AND DANCE WITH THE OBJECT OF ONE'S DESIRE IS A HIT-OR-MISS AFFAIR.

MORE THAN A FEW GET TOTALLY SHUT DOWN IN THE ATTEMPT, WHILE OTHERS NERVOUSLY NE- GOTIATE THEIR WAY THROUGH ACTUAL CONVERSATIONS AND THE EVENTUAL REWARD OF A SLOW DANCE, OR, IF EXTREMELY LUCKY, *AN ENTIRE EVENING* OF SLOW DANCES WITH THEIR NEW PARTNER.

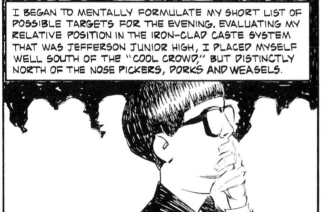

I BEGAN TO MENTALLY FORMULATE MY SHORT LIST OF POSSIBLE TARGETS FOR THE EVENING. EVALUATING MY RELATIVE POSITION IN THE IRON-CLAD CASTE SYSTEM THAT WAS JEFFERSON JUNIOR HIGH, I PLACED MYSELF WELL SOUTH OF THE "COOL CROWD," BUT DISTINCTLY NORTH OF THE NOSE PICKERS, DORKS AND WEASELS.

CHEERLEADERS, NEEDLESS TO SAY, WERE DEFINITELY UNTOUCHABLE FROM MY POS- ITION IN THE PECKING ORDER.

WHO YA CHECKIN' OUT?

SEVERAL POSSIBILITIES. DON'T KNOW YET.

WHAT ABOUT BONNIE HYSE? YOU'VE BEEN STUCK ON HER SINCE FOURTH GRADE! 'BOUT TIME YOU MADE YOUR MOVE ON HER, ROBBIE-BOY!!

I DON'T KNOW...

CHICKEN SHIT! C'MON! JUST LOOK AT HER! YOU CAN TELL SHE WANTS IT!

IT'S TRUE. SHE DOES.

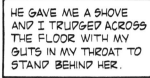

SO WHAT ARE YA WAITING FOR?

NOTHING... I'M JUST WAITING.

CHICKEN!

AM NOT!

ARE TOO!

I JUST DON'T LIKE THIS SONG...

YOU'RE JUST *SCARED!*

DON'T SEE *YOU* ASKING ANYONE.

NOT READY.

WHY NOT?

I DON'T LIKE THIS SONG, EITHER.

CHICKEN.

AM NOT!

ARE TOO!

THE SONG PLAYED OUT AND WAS CROSS-FADED INTO JOHNNY RIVERS' "POOR SIDE OF TOWN" AS BECKER CONTINUED HIS ASSAULT ON MY FRAIL MASCULINE EGO.

NEW SONG...

I KNOW.

ASK HER!

OK! I *WILL!*

NOW!

OK!

OK!

HE GAVE ME A SHOVE AND I TRUDGED ACROSS THE FLOOR WITH MY GUTS IN MY THROAT TO STAND BEHIND HER.

MY GREETING CAME OUT AS A GUTTURAL CROAK.

HI.

SHE TURNED QUICKLY AND LOCKED A STARE ON ME. I TOOK IN HER GENUINE BEAUTY FOR JUST AN INSTANT AND SUMMONED ALL MY NERVE.

WANNA DANCE?

TIME STOOD STILL.

THEN A GAZE OF ICE FROZE HER FEATURES AS SHE REPLIED IN A COLD, FLAT MONOTONE.

NO, THANK YOU.

WHERE THE STRENGTH IN ONE'S KNEES GOES AT SUCH MOMENTS IS A QUESTION FOR GREATER SCIENTIFIC MINDS THAN MINE. SUFFICE IT TO SAY THAT I STUMBLED AWAY A SHATTERED LAD AS BONNIE QUICKLY TURNED BACK TO HER FRIENDS AND ALL BROKE INTO GIGGLES.

THAT BITCH!! *SCREW* HER!!!! WHO THE HELL DOES SHE THINK SHE IS?! LET'S GO WRITE SOME STUFF ABOUT HER IN THE BATHROOM!!

FORGET IT.

AWASH IN SELF PITY, IT DIDN'T OCCUR TO ME THAT I'D PLAYED OUT APPROXIMATELY THE SAME SCENE WITH TRUDY AND MARLEEN JUST THIRTY MINUTES PRIOR. CARELESS CRUELTY WAS APPARENTLY NOT THE EXCLUSIVE PROVINCE OF EITHER GENDER AT AGE FOURTEEN.

I WAS CRUSHED. TOTALLY SHUT DOWN. I STOOD THERE LIKE A ZOMBIE, STEWING IN THOUGHTS OF REVENGE FOR THE NEXT TEN MINUTES WHILE D.J. CONTINUED SPORADIC EFFORTS TO CHEER ME UP.

"PHASE 2: THE CAUTIOUS APPROACH" HAD CULMINATED IN PERSONAL DISASTER. AS A RESULT, I WAS UNAWARE AS WE ENTERED "PHASE 3: LAST DITCH DESPERATION TIME." IT WAS NOW OR NEVER. REPUTATIONS WERE ON THE LINE. SEVERAL FAST SONGS BLASTED THROUGH THE SPEAKERS AND ECHOED AGAINST THE SCATTERED CLUSTERS, BUT THE TIME FOR LINE DANCING HAD PASSED AND BOYS AND GIRLS ALIKE PLOTTED IN EARNEST, IGNORING THEIR SIREN CALL.

I CONTINUED WITH MY IMPRESSION, "ROYAL GUARD OF BUCKINGHAM PALACE," AS D.J. RESIGNED HIMSELF; I HAD A WORLD-CLASS SULK GOING AND NO AMOUNT OF BOLSTERING WAS GOING TO HASTEN ITS PASSAGE.

HI, GUYS!

IT WAS MICHELLE GARIGAL. D.J. AND I TOOK ALGEBRA WITH HER.

HI.

HI.

GREAT DANCE, HUH? IT'S A SHAME THESE THINGS ONLY LAST TWO HOURS. I JUST LOVE THE MUSIC!

SHE SEEMED TO BE AIMING THE COMMENTS AT ME, RATHER THAN D.J.

I PICKED UP ON THIS BUT RESOLVED THAT, AS NICE A KID AS MICHELLE WAS, SHE WAS STILL NO SUB-STITUTE FOR THE ICE-QUEEN, BONNIE HYSE.

I CAME WITH KARLA BORDON. YOU KNOW KARLA, ROB...SHE SITS NEXT TO YOU IN MR. PIERCE'S SPEECH CLASS?

SUDDENLY IT CLICKED! MICHELLE WAS ACTING AS AN ADVANCE SCOUT. "ADVANCE SCOUT" WAS A TIME-HONORED TRADITION IN THE ADOLESCENT NETWORK WHERE ONE GIRL WOULD SEND A FRIEND TO DRUM UP INTEREST AND GREASE THE WHEELS FOR AN ENCOUNTER.

SURE, I KNOW KARLA. NICE GIRL...

THEN WHY DON'T YOU ASK HER TO DANCE, DUMMY! SHE'S BEEN WATCH-ING YOU WANDER AROUND ALL NIGHT AND YOU HAVEN'T EVEN COME OVER TO SAY HELLO!

UH...WELL, WE'VE BEEN KINDA BUSY... BUT, SURE! SURE, I WILL!

GET MOVIN', ROMEO!!

HEY, YOU'VE BEEN EYEING UP MICHELLE ALL NIGHT. IT'S ABOUT TIME YOU DID SOME DANCING YOURSELF, MR. B.!

NOW, "CHERISH" WAS THE QUEEN MOTHER OF ALL SLOW DANCE SONGS. SO ROMANTIC AND MELODIC WAS THIS SONG THAT IT ALMOST DEFIED ITS LISTENERS NOT TO FEEL DEEPLY IN LOVE WHILE IT ENFOLDED THEM.

POTENT SEXUAL NERVE-GAS WAFTED THROUGH THE GYM AS COUPLES ACROSS THE FLOOR BEGAN DISCREETLY NECKING. CHAPERONES AND SCHOOL OFFICIALS, MINDFUL OF DECORUM AND RAGING ADOLESCENT HORMONES, SCRAMBLED ONTO THE MORE BLATANT OFFENDERS, BUT THE COLLECTIVE MAKE-OUT SPREAD LIKE WILDFIRE.

I HAD TO SEIZE THE OPPORTUNITY. THIS SONG WOULDN'T COME AGAIN AND IT WOULD BE OVER IN A MATTER OF SECONDS! I SMILED DOWN AND SLOWLY DREW MY FACE TOWARD HER UPTURNED LIPS.

THEN, INCREDIBLY, I WAS KISSING KARLA BORDEN SQUARE ON THE MOUTH AS WE STOOD ON THE FREE-THROW LINE, EMBRACING. SHE WAS JUST SLIPPING HER TONGUE BETWEEN MY TEETH WHEN BOPPIN' BOBBY CUT INTO THE SONG WITH *THIS* WONDERFUL LITTLE PUBLIC SERVICE ANNOUNCEMENT—

ROB MAISCH! ROB MAISCH! IF THERE'S A ROB MAISCH IN THE GYM—

—YOUR FATHER IS HERE TO PICK YOU UP!!

ALL THE BLOOD DRAINED FROM MY HEAD AND I FELT LIKE I WAS GOING TO THROW UP. KARLA GIGGLED AND SMILED AS SHE STEPPED BACK FROM ME AND DRANK IN MY HORROR.

AT FOURTEEN, IT WAS BAD ENOUGH TO HAVE PARENTS; IT WAS SOCIAL SUICIDE TO HAVE THEM CALLING FOR YOU IN THE MIDST OF YOUR PEER GROUP!

BUT THERE STOOD MY FATHER IN HIS PORK PIE HAT, POWDER BLUE WINDBREAKER AND BAGGY CHECKED PANTS ATOP THE DJ STAND WHERE *EVERYONE WAS LOOKING AT HIM* AS HE SEARCHED FOR *ME* IN THE CROWD.!!

HE WAS TEN FUCKING MINUTES EARLY FOR CHRIST'S SAKE.!!!

KARLA GAVE ME AN UNDERSTANDING LOOK WHICH ONLY MADE ME FEEL WORSE.

SEE YOU IN CLASS.

GREAT TIMING!

I TOLD HIM TO WAIT OUTSIDE IN THE CAR LIKE THE REST OF THE PARENTS.

WE FOLLOWED MY DAD OUT TO THE TAN 1962 BUICK LESABRE WHILE HE GRIPED ABOUT MISSING THE BEGINNING OF THE ELEVEN O'CLOCK NEWS. AS WE MOVED THROUGH THE COLD OCTOBER NIGHT, BECKER AND I SAT SILENTLY IN THE BACK SEAT RE-RUNNING ALL THE EVENTS OF THAT FALL EVENING AND ALL THE PLANS WE HAD FOR THE DAYS AHEAD.

END

5.

10-31-94

LET ME BE CLEAR— I HATED HIS GUTS. NO QUESTION. SO DID EVERY OTHER KID IN THE NEIGHBOR-HOOD. THE THING WAS— HE HATED OURS FIRST!

MEAN OLD MAN

Rand Holmes.

MYRON

MYRON ROBBINS' GIANT HOUSE STOOD ACROSS FROM MY SMALL ONE ON CASTLE DRIVE AND HE'D LIVED THERE, ENTRENCHED, WITH HIS WIFE AND TWO DAUGHTERS SINCE THE BEGINNING OF TIME.

KEEP OFF THE GRASS

NORMAL KIDS WERE JUST TOO LOUD AND RAMBUNCTIOUS FOR MR. ROBBINS. HE'D CALL THE POLICE IF WE PLAYED STREET FOOTBALL; THE PAPER BOY GOT REAMED IF THE *DETROIT FREE PRESS* DIDN'T LAND SQUARE ON HIS DOORMAT.

CO-EXISTENCE WITH THE OLD BASTARD REQUIRED OUR RESTRAINT SINCE WE ALL HAD PARENTS. WE WERE SOLDIERS RESIGNED TO AN UNEASY OCCUPATION MADE INTERESTING ONLY BY THE INTERMITTENT SKIRMISH WITH THE ENEMY FOLLOWED BY FULL SCALE RETREAT.

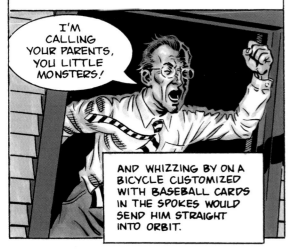

I'M CALLING YOUR PARENTS, YOU LITTLE MONSTERS!

KEEP OFF THE GRASS

TAC TAC TAC!!

AND WHIZZING BY ON A BICYCLE CUSTOMIZED WITH BASEBALL CARDS IN THE SPOKES WOULD SEND HIM STRAIGHT INTO ORBIT.

GOD, IT'S BEAUTIFUL!

IT WAS, TOO. THREE DAYS OF BUTT-BUSTING WORK HAD PAID OFF. IT WAS THE SUMMER OF '65 AND ASIDE FROM BEATLES RECORDS AND SLOT CARS, GO-CARTS WERE THE COOLEST OF ALL KID DESIRABLES.

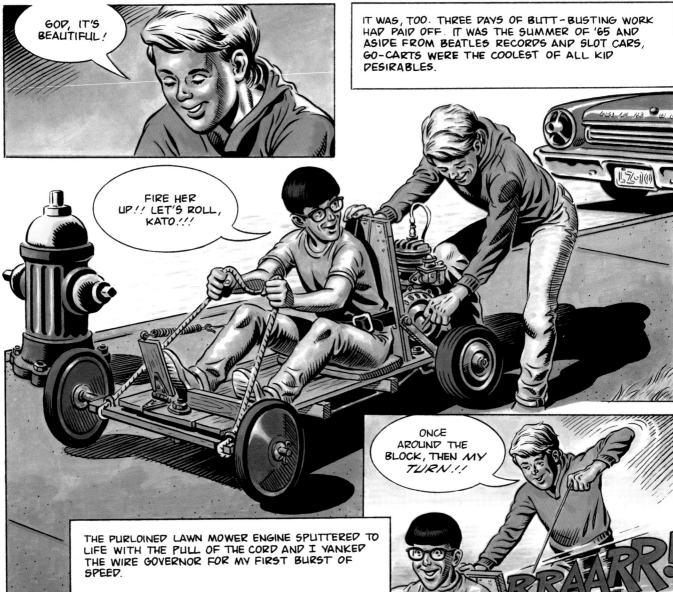

FIRE HER UP!! LET'S ROLL, KATO!!!

ONCE AROUND THE BLOCK, THEN *MY TURN!!*

THE PURLOINED LAWN MOWER ENGINE SPUTTERED TO LIFE WITH THE PULL OF THE CORD AND I YANKED THE WIRE GOVERNOR FOR MY FIRST BURST OF SPEED.

RRAARR!

THE RICKETY CRAFT TOPPED OUT AT 10 OR 12 MILES PER HOUR, BUT IN MY MIND I WAS PARNELLY JONES AT INDY! WIND IN MY FACE, I WRESTLED THE ERSATZ ROPE STEERING MECHANISM WE'D RIGGED, AND GLORIED IN THE RIDE!

THERE, JUST AHEAD, STOOD THE OFFICIAL WAVING THE CHECKERED FLAG! SOON THE ADORING RACE CROWD WOULD RUN OUT OF THE STANDS TO CONGRATULATE THIS VALIANT WHEEL WARRIOR!

SUDDENLY, I WAS BACK ON MY STREET AS I REALIZED THAT THE RACE OFFICIAL I'D JUST PASSED LOOKED SUSPICIOUSLY LIKE MR. ROBBINS IN A RED RAGE.

I ROUNDED THE CORNER AND BROUGHT THE VEHICLE TO A STOP USING THE TIME-HONORED METHOD OF RUNNING INTO THE FIRE HYDRANT IN FRONT OF BECKER'S HOUSE.

SINCE MY EARS WERE STILL BONGING FROM THE ROAR OF THE LAWNMOWER ENGINE, I HAD TO TAKE D.J.'S WORD FOR IT THAT HE COULD HEAR POLICE SIRENS GETTING CLOSER BY THE SECOND.

GROUNDED. FOR ONE WEEK. ROBBINS CALLED EVERYBODY: THE COPS, MY PARENTS, BECKER'S PARENTS. HE TOLD ANYBODY HE COULD COLLAR. HE PROBABLY PRAYED TO GOD FOR MY EVER-LASTING INCARCERATION IN HELL.

FOUR DAYS INTO MY SENTENCE, MOM RELENTED AND ALLOWED A VISITOR. JEFF MORTON ARRIVED JUST AS SHE WAS TAKING OFF FOR HER MONTHLY LIBERAL ARTS CLUB MEETING.

WITH THE WARDEN GONE, I WAS ABLE TO MAKE THE CALL TO THE SALVATION ARMY I'D BEEN PLANNING.

HALF AN HOUR LATER WE WERE POSITIONED ON THE FRONT PORCH WITH A BOX OF MOON PIES WATCHING THE TRUCK PULL UP IN FRONT OF THE ROBBINS' RESIDENCE. BEFORE LONG THE BURLY DRIVER AND HIS SIDEKICK WERE HARD AT WORK.

THE PATIO GLIDER WENT FIRST, THEN TWO PADDED LAWN CHAIRS, FOLLOWED BY AN UMBRELLAED PICNIC TABLE.

THEY SHOULD HAVE BROUGHT A BIGGER TRUCK. HERE COMES THE GRILL.

SUDDENLY ROBBINS' TAN FORD FAIRLANE ROUNDED THE CORNER AND SCREECHED TO A HALT BEHIND THE SALVATION ARMY TRUCK JUST AS THE WORKMEN WERE LOADING THE WEBER GRILL.

UH-OH.

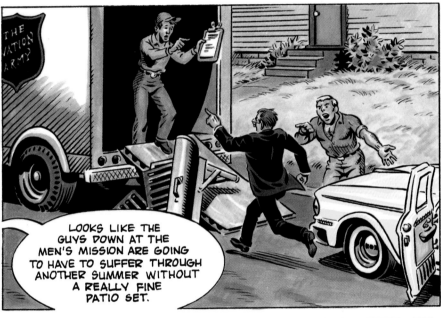

LOOKS LIKE THE GUYS DOWN AT THE MEN'S MISSION ARE GOING TO HAVE TO SUFFER THROUGH ANOTHER SUMMER WITHOUT A REALLY FINE PATIO SET.

NO, MR. ROBBINS, HE'S GROUNDED. HE'S NOT ALLOWED TO USE THE PHONE. I THINK YOU SHOULD CALL SOMEBODY ELSE'S PARENTS FOR A CHANGE. GOOD-BYE.

WERE YOU BOYS ON THE PHONE THIS AFTERNOON?

NOPE... GROUNDED, REMEMBER?

YES, I DO. YOU CAN TACK THREE MORE DAYS ON TO YOUR SENTENCE, BUSTER.

WHAT FOR??!!

GOOD MEASURE.

SIX EXCRUCIATINGLY BORING DAYS LATER.

SINCE I WAS HIS ARCH NEMESIS HE WOULD BE QUICK TO BLAME ME FOR ANY RETALIATION. THEREFORE, A SCHEDULE OF "HITS" WAS WORKED OUT TO COINCIDE WITH MY DOWN TIME AT HOME.

TIME IN WHICH I WAS DETERMINED TO BE AS CONSPICUOUS AS POSSIBLE.

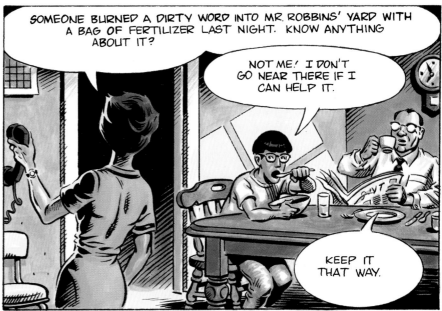

EVEN THE LOCAL ADULTS WERE AMUSED THE FOLLOWING WEEK WHEN A DERELICT COMMODE APPEARED IN THE CENTER OF MYRON'S YARD PLACED ATOP AN OSCILLATING SPRINKLER HE'D LEFT RUNNING THE NIGHT BEFORE.

LESS AMUSED WERE THE HALF-DOZEN LOCAL REAL ESTATE AGENTS WHO HAD TO GO TO ROBBINS' TO RETRIEVE TWENTY-EIGHT "FOR SALE" SIGNS THAT HAD BEEN SWIPED FROM HOUSES IN A TEN BLOCK RADIUS AND PLANTED EN-MASSE LIKE ROWS OF CORN.

MY PARENTS FIELDED MORE ANGRY CALLS AS THE REIGN OF TERROR CONTINUED BUT MY ALIBIS WERE ALWAYS IRON-CLAD.

THEN, ONE DAY IN LATE AUGUST, D.J. AND I WERE SITTING IN MY FRONT YARD TRADING OUTER LIMITS CARDS WHEN WE NOTICED MR. ROBBINS PUSHING THE LAWN MOWER OUT OF HIS GARAGE.

SINCE THE FERTILIZER BURN, HE'D LET THE YARD GROW BACK FOR WELL OVER A MONTH AND THE GRASS WAS SEVEN INCHES HIGH IN SOME SPOTS.

LOOK, I'LL GIVE YOU THE DEMON AND *TWO* ZANTI MISFITS FOR YOUR "TOURIST ATTRACTION" LIZARD.

RRAARR

NO WAY!

THE SOUND WAS *INCREDIBLE!!* METAL ON METAL, LIKE A BOX OF BALL BEARINGS THROWN INTO AN OPEN TURBINE! SHRAPNEL BLEW OUT OF THE GRASS CHUTE IN A FAN, ONE PIECE MAKING A DIRECT HIT ON A BEDROOM WINDOW AND BREAKING A ONE-INCH THERMAL PANE.

SMASH

YAAAA!!!

KKKRRAAKKRR KKRRAANNG KRR

AS SOON AS HE COULD GET NEAR ENOUGH, ROBBINS SHUT DOWN THE MOWER AND KNELT IN THE GRASS.

WHAT'S HE DOING?

UH-OH.

YOU DID IT !!!! ADMIT IT, YOU BRAT !!!

I DIDN'T DO ANYTHING, MR. ROBBINS.

OH, IT'S MISTER WIDE-EYED AND INNOCENT AGAIN!

I'M SURE YOU WERE WATCHING TV WITH YOUR DADDY WHILE YOUR PALS DID YOUR DIRTY WORK!!

YES, YOU!! EVERY KID I KNOW HATES YOUR LIVING GUTS!!!! YOU WANNA KNOW WHY?!!

WHY DON'T YOU JUST LAY OFF, MR. ROBBINS?!! YOU'RE THE ONE WHO STARTED ALL THIS STUFF!!

ME?!!

BECAUSE YOU'RE A MEAN OLD MAN!!!

FOR THE FIRST AND ONLY TIME IN MY MEMORY, MYRON ROBBINS HAD NOTHING TO SAY. HE JUST STOOD THERE LOOKING AT ME FOR THIRTY OR FORTY SECONDS.

THEN HE WALKED BACK TO HIS HOUSE AND WENT INSIDE.

WHAT THE HELL HAPPENED OVER THERE?

TOM AND PAGE STOLE A KEG OF NAILS. THEY PEPPERED MYRON'S WHOLE FRONT LAWN WITH 'EM LAST NIGHT.

JESUS, THIS HAS GONE TOO DAMN FAR. IT'S GOT TO STOP.

I WAITED FOR THE PHONE CALL TO MY PARENTS FOR THREE DAYS BUT IT NEVER CAME. NOR DID THE POLICE ARRIVE ON ANY NEIGHBORHOOD DOORSTEPS LOOKING FOR CULPRITS. MR. ROBBINS' HAD DISAPPEARED INTO HIS HOUSE AND I WOULD NOT SEE HIM AGAIN FOR MANY WEEKS.

IN EARLY OCTOBER WE WATCHED TWO MAYFLOWER MOVING MEN COMPLETE THE PACKING OF THE ROBBINS' HOUSE WITH THE GLIDER, PADDED LAWN CHAIRS AND UMBRELLAED PICNIC TABLE FROM THE BACK PATIO. I LOOKED OVER AT BECKER AND MORTON WITH A SMILE. MORTON READ MY MIND AND LAUGHED.

I DIDN'T CALL THEM. DID *YOU* CALL THEM?

AS THE HUGE SEMI PULLED AWAY, MYRON ROBBINS, WITH WIFE AND CHILDREN IN TOW, EMERGED FROM HIS CASTLE AND WALKED TO THE FAIRLANE.

HE LOOKED BACK AT THE HOUSE FOR A FEW SECONDS WHILE HIS FAMILY BUCKLED UP. THEN HE GOT IN AND STARTED THE ENGINE.

AND THEN THEY WERE GOING. AS THE FORD SLOWLY PASSED US THAT DAY I COULDN'T HELP WAVING GOOD-BYE.

NOT TO BE A SMART-ASS OR TO FEIGN FRIENDLINESS. BUT, AS A SHOW OF RESPECT FOR A DEFEATED ENEMY.

END

GRIFFIN LOVE and the HOOKER

GRIF LOVE WAS A WISE-ASS UNDERACHIEVER WITH A REAL TASTE FOR SOPHOMORIC PRANKS. NEEDLESS TO SAY, HE WAS A VERY POPULAR GUY.

THE OCCASIONAL CATASTROPHIC REPORT CARD CONTAINING TEACHERS' COMMENTS RANGING FROM "YOUR SON IS A MONSTER" TO "PLEASE KILL THIS BOY" ONLY STRENGTHENED HIS FAMILY'S RESOLVE TO STAND BY HIM.

AND, OF COURSE, THE DEAN OF BOYS WAS A GREAT SUPPORTER AND CONFIDANTE.

KLINGON BATTLE HELMET

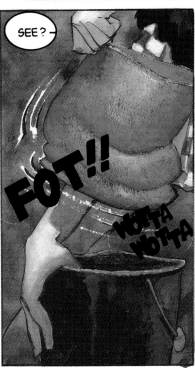

THE GLORIOUS DAY FINALLY ARRIVES.

GOT ANY *REAL* TRIBBLES?!

THEY GOT TONS RIGHT HERE, BUDDY, BUT YOU BETTER ACT FAST, 'CAUSE I'M STOCKING UP.' THEY'RE SWELL.

THEY SUCK.

FOR YOUR INFORMATION, *BUDDY*—A. THOSE THINGS ARE MADE OUT OF CARPET SCRAPS, **B.** THEY FALL APART IN A WEEK AND **C.** YOU CAN GET 'EM FOR HALF THAT PRICE AT THE PIGGLY-WIGGLY.

I COLLECT ONLY *GENUINE* STAR TREK STUFF.

WHAT YOU *SEE* IS WHAT WE *GOT.'*

: SIGH :

HOW GOES IT BACK HERE?

NOT GOOD. THAT KID HAS BEEN A MAJOR PAIN IN THE ASS ALL DAY.

WHICH ONE?

MR. AUTHORITY OVER THERE. THE ONE TELLING EVERYBODY IN THE PLACE NOT TO BUY OUR "CHEAP CRAP."

IS THAT SO?

WELL, WELL.

6:00. CLOSING TIME.

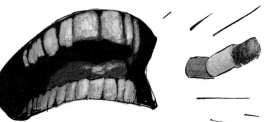

SHOW'S OVER, FLY-SPECKS! OUT OF THE POOL! C'MON YOU LOSERS, HAUL YOUR BUTTS!!

ALL, THAT IS, WITH ONE EXCEPTION.

WHA..?

YOU IMPRESS ME AS A MAN WHO WANTS TO BE AT THE VERY TOP OF HIS HOBBY.

HOBBY?! IT'S A WAY OF LIFE, MAN!!

I HAVE AN ITEM I THINK YOU'LL WANT TO SEE.

WHA... WHAT ITEM?

MR. MAISCH, COULD YOU JOIN US IN THE BACK PARLOR?

MOST ASSUREDLY, MR. CROOKSTON.

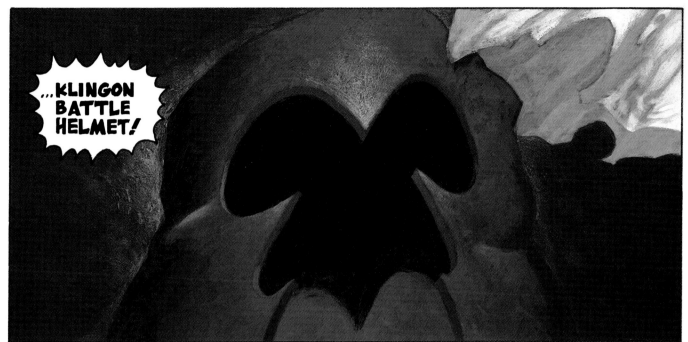

PANT!
PANT!

FIFTY BUCKS.

GASP! CHOKE!

I ONLY GOT $37.50.

≻SIGH≺ SHOW ME.

HM.

OK. $37.50, THEN.

SNATCH

STUFF STUFF

NOW, LISTEN CAREFULLY. EVERYBODY WHO WAS HERE TODAY WOULD BE PISSED THAT I DIDN'T GIVE THEM A SHOT AT THIS, SO YOU'VE GOT TO KEEP YOUR TRAP SHUT. NEVER TELL ANYBODY WHERE YOU GOT THIS!

THAT'S THE DEAL.

THE INTERCOM BUZZER ON MY OFFICE PHONE HUMMED TWO CYCLES BEFORE I LAID MY COPY OF "SHOPPING CENTER WORLD" MAGAZINE ASIDE AND PICKED UP THE HANDSET.

WHAT'S UP, BABS?

YOU AREN'T GOING TO BELIEVE THIS. ARNOLD NESBITT, THE SEGMENT PRODUCER OF THE "AMERICAN FOLKS" TELEVISION PROGRAM IS CALLING FROM LOS ANGELES ON LINE TWO!

NO SHIT? HE PROBABLY WANTS ME FOR THE "PRIMO HUNKS OF '81" SEGMENT!

JUST PICK UP THE LINE, MR. HOLLYWOOD! {CLICK}

MR. MAISCH?

YES, MR. NESBITT, HOW CAN I HELP YOU?

I UNDERSTAND YOUR SHOPPING CENTER IS BRINGING IN BRODY SLADE OF THE OLD "THUNDER RIDER" TELEVISION SERIES FOR A WESTERN PROMOTION.

YES, HE'LL BE HERE IN THE AFTERNOON ON SATURDAY THE 22ND FOR AN ON-STAGE AND AUTOGRAPH SESSION.

WITH YOUR PERMISSION, I'D LIKE TO BRING OUR HOST POLLY WHITEHEAD, AND A CREW OUT TO YOUR MALL TO FILM A "WHERE ARE THEY NOW?" SEGMENT FOR OUR FALL PREMIERE EDITION OF "AMERICAN FOLKS."

IT HAS THAT GREAT HUMAN INTEREST ANGLE. "WHAT'S BECOME OF ONE OF THE MOST POPULAR TEENAGE STARS OF 40'S SERIALS AND 50'S TELEVISION NOW THAT HIS FAME IS TWENTY-FIVE YEARS GONE."

FREE PUBLICITY! FREE NATIONAL PUBLICITY!, MY BRAIN SCREAMED!

WE'D LOVE TO HAVE YOU HERE FOR BRODY SLADE'S SHOW, MR. NESBITT!

GREAT. WE'D LIKE TO INTERVIEW HIM AND WE'VE WORKED THAT END OUT WITH HIS AGENT, RONNIE SHEEN. MOSTLY, WE WANT TO FILM HIM ON STAGE—TALKING WITH KIDS, LISTENING TO THEIR PARENTS GUSH ABOUT THE OLD SHOW.

WARM, FUZZY STUFF LIKE THAT, YA' KNOW? NOSTALGIC AS HELL!

AFTER NESBITT TOOK HIMSELF OFF TO WHEEL HIS NEXT DEAL, I JUST KICKED BACK FOR FIVE MINUTES AND BASKED IN MY GOOD FORTUNE.

THOUSANDS OF DOLLARS IN FREE PUBLICITY WAS *THE* KEY TO SUCCESS IN MALL MARKETING.

IT WAS ALSO A STRONG FACTOR IN GETTING NOTICED BY THE INTERNATIONAL COUNCIL OF SHOPPING CENTER'S MAXI AWARDS JUDGES.

I'D ALSO LIKE TO THANK...

AND BRODY SLADE, A HAS-BEEN WESTERN HERO, WAS MY TICKET TO RIDE.

I THOUGHT ABOUT THE GRAINY BLACK AND WHITE SERIES THAT HAD BEEN A WEEKLY STAPLE OF MY CHILDHOOD.

WHAT SET IT APART WAS THAT THE THUNDER RIDER WAS ONLY 18 YEARS OLD; THE BAD GUYS ALWAYS UNDERESTIMATED HIM, CALLED HIM A "PUNK KID."

AT WHICH POINT, OF COURSE, HE ALWAYS KICKED THEIR ASS. AND, OF COURSE, I ATE IT UP—ALONG WITH THE BLAMMO-PUFFS CEREAL AND PECOS-ADE JUICE DRINK HE ALWAYS HAWKED DURING COMMERCIALS.

I REMEMBER CAJOLING MY POOR FAMILY INTO EATING BUCKETS OF THAT SAWDUST-CEREAL SO I COULD GET ENOUGH PROOFS-OF-PURCHASE TO SEND OFF FOR A TIN *JUNIOR THUNDER RIDER DEPUTY* BADGE.

THEN THERE WAS THE THUNDER RIDER COSTUME MY MOTHER MADE FOR ME WHEN I WAS FIVE. THE REAL THUNDER RIDER WAS CLAD IN BLACK FROM HEAD TO FOOT WITH A FLOWING CAPE AND A GOLDEN THUNDERBOLT EMBLAZONED ON HIS CHEST. A FULL-FACE MESH NET MASK HID HIS TRUE IDENTITY.

THIS ENSEMBLE WAS TOPPED WITH A BLACK HAT SPORTING FEATHER PLUMES WHICH, IN RETROSPECT, LOOKED MORE LIKE A GAY PIRATE'S HEADGEAR THAN A COWBOY'S STETSON.

MOM TACKLED THE COSTUME WITH TYPICAL MOM-ZEAL, FASHIONING THE OUTFIT FROM A BLACK, GIRL'S LEOTARD, A BIG OLD CLOTH CHURCH HAT AND MOTH-EATEN CURTAINS DIPPED IN BLACK RIT DYE.

THE FOOT AND CALF OF A PAIR OF BLACK NYLON STOCKINGS COMPLETED THE EFFECT.

WHEN I PROUDLY DONNED MY NEW COSTUME ON HALLOWEEN NIGHT, 1957, MY FATHER LOOKED UP FROM HIS "MIDLAND DAILY NEWS" AND SAID, "MY GOD, MADGE! HE LOOKS LIKE HEDDA HOPPER AT A FUNERAL!"

HI, BRODY. LOOKING FORWARD TO HAVING YOU HERE IN DALLAS.

YEAH. SO, YOU'RE GETTIN' ME A HORSE FOR THIS "AMERICAN FOLKS" TV SHOW?

YES, I—

LOOK, KID, I ONLY RIDE ONE HORSE. HIS NAME'S SLIM. HE'S BOARDED OUT AT HAMPTON FARMS, SOUTH OF ARLINGTON. YOU GET *THAT* HORSE! NO SUBSTITUTES!

HORSES ARE SNEAKY, UNPREDICTABLE BASTARDS.

OKAY, I'LL GIVE THEM A CALL.

YOU GET *THAT* HORSE! NO OTHER... OR I *DON'T RIDE*!!!

WILL THERE BE ANYTHING ELSE?

I WAS TRYING NOT TO SOUND TOO DEPRESSED.

YEAH, THE LIMO! IT'S GOT TO BE *BLACK*!! I DON'T RIDE IN ANY SISSY WHITE LIMOS!! GOT IT?

I DON'T THINK IT'LL BE A PROBLEM, BRODY.

GOOD! SLIM THE HORSE AND BLACK THE LIMOUSINE! IF YOU DON'T SCREW THOSE UP, WE'LL GET ALONG JUST FINE!

I'LL PICK YOU UP AT THE AIRPORT ON THE EVENING OF THE 21ST.

CLICK

TWO HOURS AND TWO ASPIRINS LATER I ARRIVED AT HAMPTON FARMS.

A BEAUTIFUL ANIMAL. PUREBRED, YOU KNOW.

I STEPPED CAREFULLY IN ANKLE-HIGH HAY TO AVOID GETTING HORSE SHIT ALL OVER MY TASSELED BLACK LOAFERS.

IT'S AN AFTERNOON SHOW. WE BASICALLY JUST NEED SLIM AT THE BEGINNING FOR BRODY SLADE'S ENTRANCE.

NO PROBLEM. WE CAN TRAILER HIM TO YOUR PARKING LOT AND SADDLE UP THERE.

WHAT'S THE FEE FOR HIS RENTAL?

WE CAN DO IT FOR $2,500.

TWENTY-FIVE HUNDRED DOLLARS?!"

THAT'S HIGHWAY ROBBERY!!!!

YEP. BUT I KNOW THAT BRODY SLADE WON'T RIDE ANY OTHER HORSE, SO YOU'RE STUCK WITH US...OR NOTHING.

AS I DROVE AWAY, LIGHT ONE $2500 CHECK FOR SERVICES TO BE RENDERED, I TRIED TO FORGET THE CRACK-WIDENING I'D JUST RECEIVED AND CONCENTRATE ON THE FUTURE.

NATIONAL PUBLICITY. NATIONAL PUBLICITY.

SLADE HAD BEEN MADE AVAILABLE TO US THROUGH A GROUP DEAL IN WHICH HE WOULD APPEAR AT TEN OF OUR COMPANY'S MALLS FOR A FLAT FEE SPLIT TEN WAYS. PHONE CALLS FROM OTHER MARKETING DIRECTORS WHO'D HOSTED HIM EARLY IN THE TOUR CONFIRMED WHAT AN ASSHOLE I SUSPECTED HIM TO BE.

DOWN DEEP, I STEELED MYSELF FOR THE ORDEAL I KNEW WAS LANDING ON MY DOORSTEP IN A FEW SHORT WEEKS.

IT WAS A STEAMY 87 DEGREES AS I ARRIVED BY BLACK LIMOUSINE AT THE AMERICAN AIRLINES TERMINAL OF DFW AT HALF PAST NINE ON THE EVENING OF AUGUST 21ST.

FIVE MINUTES AFTER EVERYONE ELSE HAD DEBARKED, BRODY SLADE EMERGED FROM THE SHELTER OF THE PLANE WITH A DUFFEL BAG CLUTCHED TIGHTLY IN HIS HAND AND A SPORT COAT DRAPED OVER HIS HEAD.

HE HURLED HIMSELF INTO THE REAR SEAT NEXT TO ME AND DIDN'T REMOVE THE COAT FROM HIS FACE UNTIL THE DRIVER HAD CLOSED THE DOOR.

DAMN PRESS PHOTOGRAPHERS! THEY'RE EVERY-WHERE, YA KNOW? JUST DYING TO GET A PICTURE OF ME OUT OF COSTUME.

THEY DO THE SAME THING TO *KISS* WHEN THEY'RE OFF-STAGE!

DID YOU GET THE HORSE?

I COULDN'T HELP WINCING AT THE MEMORY OF THE $2,500 TAB FOR OLD SLIM.

ALL SET. NO PROBLEM. HOW WAS YOUR FLIGHT?

OUTSTANDING! TAKE IT FROM ME, SON, THOSE STEWS KNOW HOW TO TREAT A CELEBRITY. YESSIREEBOB.

SPEAKIN' OF WHICH, WHERE WOULD AN OLD COWBOY FIND A LITTLE FEMALE COMPANIONSHIP FOR THE EVENING? I HEAR DALLAS GALS ARE SUPPOSED TO BE ALL-NIGHT RIDERS.

I DON'T HAVE THE SLIGHTEST IDEA.

YOU DON'T GET OUT MUCH, DO YA, PARD?

BY THE TIME THE LIMO PULLED UP IN FRONT OF THE QUIMBY SUITES HOTEL, I'D HAD MORE THAN MY FILL OF OLD BRODY, THANKS. ALL I WANTED WAS TO SHAKE THIS DOG SHIT OFF MY SHOE AND GO HOME.

CAREFUL WITH THAT! I'VE GOT THE THUNDERSWORD IN THERE!

WE'RE EN ROUTE NOW, SIR. I'M CALLING FROM THE CAR PHONE. I WANTED TO LET YOU KNOW THAT IT MIGHT BE A GOOD IDEA TO HAVE SOME COFFEE WAITING FOR MR. SLADE WHEN HE GETS THERE.

OH, MAN. WHAT HAPPENED?

APPARENTLY, MR. SLADE HAD A BIT TOO MUCH FUN AFTER WE LEFT HIM LAST NIGHT. WE'VE SPENT THE LAST 45 MINUTES GETTING HIM DRESSED AND INTO THE CAR.

WHO THE HELL IS "WE?"

A MISS BABS AND A MAID NAMED TRIXIE. THEY WERE ALL IN HIS BED WHEN I ARRIVED AT HIS ROOM TO COLLECT HIM. HE WAS USING THE MAID'S FEATHER DUSTER TO—

I DON'T WANT TO KNOW! JUST GET HIM OVER HERE IN ONE PIECE!

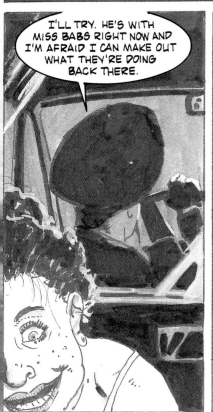

I'LL TRY. HE'S WITH MISS BABS RIGHT NOW AND I'M AFRAID I CAN MAKE OUT WHAT THEY'RE DOING BACK THERE.

TURN A COLD HOSE ON THEM IF YOU HAVE TO! JUST MAKE SURE THEY'RE NOT *CONNECTED* BY THE TIME YOU ARRIVE HERE, IF YOU GET MY DRIFT. THERE'S A BIG TIP IN THIS FOR YOU.

THANKS FOR CALLING TO WARN ME, BRUCE.

I HUNG UP THE PHONE AND CRADLED MY HEAD IN MY HANDS.

SECURITY REPORTED THAT THE CENTER COURT CROWD NOW NUMBERED AROUND 2,000 AND THAT POLLY WHITEHEAD HAD AUTOGRAPHED HIS LOG BOOK.

G'MORNING, MR. MAISCH.

IT'S AFTERNOON, BRODY. FORTY-FIVE MINUTES TILL SHOWTIME, TO BE EXACT. HAVE SOME COFFEE AND GET INTO YOUR THUNDER RIDER COSTUME.

YOU'VE GOT 2,000 PEOPLE OUT THERE WAITING TO SEE YOU! YOU'D BETTER SOBER UP AND GET YOUR ACT TOGETHER.

NO PROBLEM. I'LL BE READY, BOSS!

HEY, DID YOU MEET BABS? WHAT A WILD WOMAN! I TOLD YOU TEXAS GALS WERE THE GREATEST!

GET HER A GOOD SEAT UP REAL CLOSE TO THE STAGE, WILL YA, PARDNER?

SECURITY IS ESCORTING HER, AS WE SPEAK.

I'D INSTRUCTED THEM TO WALK HER TO THE FAR END OF THE MALL AND THROW HER FAT ASS OUT IN THE STREET.

AT LEAST SLIM'S READY.

SLADE EMERGED FROM MY OFFICE IN FULL THUNDER RIDER REGALIA. HE ACTUALLY LOOKED PRETTY GOOD IN THE COSTUME. THE GIRDLE HID A MULTITUDE OF PHYSICAL SINS, AND I SUSPECTED HE WAS WEARING ELEVATOR BOOTS TO INCREASE HIS STATURE.

YOU LOOK GREAT, BRODY. IT'S ALMOST SHOW TIME AND YOU ARE GOING TO MEET SEVERAL THOUSAND OF YOUR ADORING TEXAS FANS! SLIM'S ALL SADDLED UP AND RARING TO GO, AND IN TWENTY-FIVE MINUTES THE LEGENDARY THUNDER RIDER WILL GALLOP INTO LONE STAR MALL!

I DON'T RIDE IN THE RAIN. I HATE WORKING IN A DAMP COSTUME. I'LL JUST WALK UP TO THE STAGE.

WHAT?!!

THE HELL YOU SAY!!! I'VE GOT TWENTY-FIVE HUNDRED DOLLARS WRAPPED UP IN THAT DAMN HORSE AND YOU ARE GOING TO RIDE LIKE THE FUCKING WIND!!!

NOT DOING IT. TALK TO RONNIE, IF YOU DON'T LIKE IT.

END

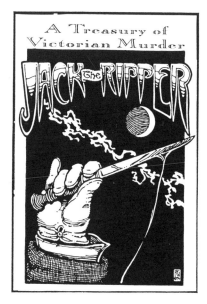